DARKSIDE SEATTLE:
STREET DOC

DARKSIDE SEATTLE:
STREET DOC

L.E. FRENCH

Published by Clockwork Dragon Books

clockworkdragon.net

First printing, October 2016

ISBN: 978-1-944334-12-3

For Eric, who introduced me to cyberpunk.

For Bob, Greg, and Mike, who have willingly suffered through my cyberpunk games for many moons.

CHAPTER 1

Stale sweat and thick smoke ceased to bother me after two shots of cheap whiskey. I leaned on the rough, grimy bar of yet another place I hadn't bothered to check the name of, brooding over a tumbler with two more fingers of alcohol. Maybe if I slammed all that down too, I'd pass out and wake up to discover my life hadn't been tossed into the toilet. Probably not.

Some guy in worse shape than me shuffled to the sex robot in the corner of our dimly lit hellhole and pulled its black plastic curtain shut. Tinny country music didn't block out the sound of that poor slob fucking a machine. At least he knew it was clean, I suppose. Those things self-sanitized.

I raked a hand through my short, dark hair for the five-hundredth time. By now, I had to look and smell like shit. Before blundering into this dump, I'd wandered in a daze long enough to forget what a real bed feels like. My uptight, Japanese mother would scream with rage if she saw me, and not only because my wife tossed me out and the board took away my medical license. Surgeons must be clean-shaven. Suits must be respected. Cleanliness must be upheld.

Above all, appearance.

Sipping at my whiskey, I tried to use the uplink in my head to check the time by reflex. Nothing happened. Brad, my boss, had disabled the whole implant. Never mind that I paid for the medical upgrades myself. Never mind that it did more than control diagnostic and surgical nanosuites. No, Hideo had to be punished and isolated. My access to the news and weather needed to be cut off.

Worse, I couldn't access my bank account. Three days ago, I landed in the gutter with nothing. A greasy Mexican in a pawn shop took my wedding ring for a wad of paper cash. With what I had left, I could maybe feed myself for another few days. Assuming I didn't blow it all on a bender. Maybe I could wander into a dark alley and let some gangbanger beat me up for the cred I didn't have so I could spend some time in an emergency room.

One of the four other assholes in this dive fell out of his chair and hit the sticky floor with a thump. Everyone noticed. No one cared. The bartender, a beefy man with a mohawk and clothes in better shape than mine, tossed a dingy, stained hand towel over his shoulder and approached the guy. He checked the drunk's pulse and grunted. I wish I could say it surprised me to see him rifle through the guy's pockets and take all the cash he found. Tucking a handful of bills and change into his pocket, the bartender picked up the guy's half-empty glass of crappy beer and returned to the bar.

"He dead?" I asked out of curiosity.

"Nope. Not yet."

I knocked back the rest of my whiskey, hoping it would make my brain shut up. Nothing else had worked yet. Setting the glass on the bar, I tried to figure out what to do with myself. My wife, Ai, had everything. She'd probably already filed for divorce. I could go back and contest it. Except then I'd have to stand up in a courtroom and argue about whether I could pay child support or not. I'd get arrested and nothing good would come from that.

"You want another one?" the bartender asked, already reaching for the bottle.

"No." I fished money out of my pocket and sighed at the pathetically thin stack of worn paper. Dropping a bill on the bar, I watched the bartender notice and nod at how much I thought the swill he'd served me was worth. When I stood and headed for the door, he didn't stop me, so I figured we were even.

I stepped outside and hunched my shoulders in the light rain and harsh neon of evening in Darkside Seattle. The locals called it DeeSeat. Until three long days ago, I'd only heard about this place on the news. Every day, the chipper blonde on the holoscreen started the morning by reporting about someone knifed, shot, run down, or overdosed the night before in Darkside Seattle.

Then I went to work at the most advanced surgical center in the country, where everything gleamed and sparkled. My Madison Park office floor-to-ceiling windows overlooked Lake Washington. I imagined Brad, the chief surgeon, going through my desk, tossing my stuff into a box and shoving it into storage. Or maybe he threw it all out. Hell, the bastard probably gave it to Ai.

I ignored the hookers catcalling me and the chipheads begging for a fix, a burger, or spare change. Hard plastic screens covering the walls flickered as I shuffled past, half of them broken or broadcasting static, and the other half unable to connect to my disabled 'link and pick an advertisement based on my preferences. I turned away from the random brunette shoving her airbrushed, gold-painted boobs at screen after screen. They reminded me too much of Bunny's augmented breasts.

Muffled gunshots shattered a memory of bending Bunny over my desk at work. When I looked up, I saw two men wearing black pleather trench coats with a creepy pair of eyes painted on the back stumble through a door into an alley festooned with broken crates, overfilled dumpsters, and rotting garbage. One half-carried the other. He used their bodies to shut the door and leaned against it. The other man slumped in his arms, unable to help.

Someone thumped against the door from the inside, knocking the two men to the wet concrete. My past as an emergency room doctor sent me running to their aid. Adrenaline coursing through me, I dove in head first, not giving a crap about good guy or bad guy. These men—up close, I realized they couldn't be older than twenty—needed help. Throwing myself against the door, I held it shut while someone on the inside tried to shove it open.

The one able-bodied kid patted the other down, shoving aside the shreds of a red wool scarf. At first, I thought he might be mugging the guy. Way to go, Hideo. Bravo for jumping in and doing the wrong thing. Then I saw blood smeared on his hands.

Their assailant stopped trying to open the door. I let go and lurched into a crouch beside the fallen kid. "What happened?" Shoving his hands out of the way, I probed for a wound, not sure what I could do about it under these conditions.

Brad could take away my license, but he couldn't take away the part of me that had demanded I become a doctor in the first place.

"Shot," the one kid sobbed, panic making him seem even younger than I thought. I revised my estimate of his age down to sixteen. He shrank on himself, huddling inside his trench coat. "He had a gun. We didn't think he'd have a gun."

"Where?" When the kid covered his face, I focused on finding the wound. I shoved the dying kid's coat aside and found blood on his plastic mesh shirt, then the bleeding wound in his side. At a guess, it probably hit his kidney, which he'd survive if I could stop the bleeding. Getting the bullet out in this alley seemed like a stupid idea without tools. I didn't even have a pocket knife. "What're your names?"

The kid whimpered as I revealed the injury. "We have to get out of here. Deadbolt's gonna kill us."

His panic reminded me of my four-year-old daughter when she woke up from a nightmare. Ai had much better skills at handling her terror. I only ever floundered. Hotshot surgeon man could keep his shit in the operating room, but not in the face of a little girl's tears. Out here, I had no Ai to fall back on.

"We can move him, but we'll have to be careful." I did everything in my power to scoop up the unconscious kid without making his injury worse. He weighed too much for me to move very fast. So long as we didn't have to go far, I'd manage. "Lead me someplace we'll be safe for a while and I'll help your friend."

The kid scrambled to his feet and wiped his face. "What can you do?"

The real answer? Not much. We'd probably reach a squalid dump in time to watch this poor kid die. No ambulance would get here soon enough, even if I had the ability to call for one. Looking into the other kid's eyes, seeing how much he needed his friend, I couldn't tell him that. Instead, I forced myself to pretend everything would be fine. With a determined nod, I squared my shoulders and took the first step out of the alley.

"I'm a doctor. Let's go."

CHAPTER 2

Panting and shaking, I stumbled inside an abandoned gas station. Delusion, as my guide insisted upon calling himself, slammed the door shut, throwing a cloud of dust over us. I laid Phantom on the first surface I saw, a grime-covered counter strewn with garbage. The elite surgeon in me curled my lip in disgust at the conditions I had to work under.

Checking Phantom's pulse, I found it thin but still present. This kid might make it. I stripped his coat off with care and hiked up his shirt while scanning the small cashier's office. "Delusion, I need a knife, something like tweezers, clean water, something to soak up blood, and whatever you can find to hold him together afterward. Any kind of tape or a needle and thread. Something."

Delusion produced a survival knife with a black handle and serration on the back edge. I would have preferred a scalpel. Something about beggars and choosers flitted through my mind and I took the knife. Thank goodness Phantom was already unconscious.

"I'll look around for the rest, Doc." Delusion dove into the task of searching the shelves and drawers behind the counter. He seemed happier to have a task and a way to contribute. At the least, it kept him too busy to fret.

I shucked my suit jacket and let it fall on the floor. Holding the knife, I noticed my hands shaking. The stupid disabled implant controlled all the hormones released by my emotional state to keep that from happening. I'd have to calm myself down the old-fashioned way. "No pressure," I muttered. "Just going to blind extract a bullet in a dirty shack with a dirty knife, no assistants, no nanites, and no blood transfusions."

On the bright side, if I killed Phantom, he'd be no worse off than if Delusion had dragged him home. "I hope you're healthy, kid." I took a deep breath, held the tip of a knife much too large for the job, and visualized what I meant to do.

Delusion burst in and scared the shit out of me. I dropped the knife and squealed like my daughter. Somehow, I managed not to wet my pants. Or maybe I did and couldn't tell since I was already soaked.

"I set a bowl outside to collect rainwater," Delusion said, apparently oblivious to my distress. Or maybe he didn't care. He held out a pair of needlenose pliers, an old box of feminine sanitary pads, and a roll of duct tape. "Will this stuff work?"

Picking up the knife, I nodded. Combined with a few deep breaths, crouching and straightening gave me a chance to calm down. "Set it all on the counter." While Delusion obeyed, I steeled myself to cut this kid open.

Delusion gulped and covered his eyes. "Don't kill him," he whimpered. "That's my brother."

No pressure, right? "*Chikusho,*" I breathed. Snatching up the pliers, I cringed at the amount of grease and dirt on the metal. I wiped them on my pants and hoped Phantom had gotten his tetanus booster. With a deep breath, I eased the tip of the knife into the wound. Blood filled the cavity as I cut his flesh and eased the wound open.

I waited for a nurse to do her job at the same time I waited for my implant to tell me exactly where to find the bullet. And then I scolded myself for being such a creature of habit. This problem fell on me and whatever I could convince Delusion to do. No crutches.

"Delusion, grab a pad and use it to soak up blood for me."

He gulped and followed my order. As an assistant, he could've been worse. "There's a lot of blood," he whispered.

"There's always a lot of blood." I gritted my teeth and did the damned job. When I got a grip on the bullet with the pliers, I felt a rush of victory. Then I wiggled it out of Phantom's body and wanted to whoop. I hadn't felt anything but determined and confident during a procedure since medical school. One week after I graduated, I got my emotion regulator. The upgrade had been worth it. Until now, of course.

In that moment, I hated Ai more than I'd ever hated anyone or anything before. Then I remembered I still had a patient to save. And dammit, I could do anything and save anyone with these incredible hands. With Delusion's help, I washed the wound and covered it with pads and duct tape.

Phantom's pulse remained weak but steady, and I was a god. "He still needs real medical care," I told Delusion with a grin I couldn't suppress, "but he's going to live."

Delusion hugged me and sobbed his gratitude into my bloody shirt. When he pulled away, wiping his nose, he looked up at me with wide eyes, the gaze of a child in awe of his hero. I basked in the glow. "I called for a ride," he said with a sniffle. "They'll be here soon."

"Good." Hands on my hips, I felt like a goddamned superhero. With nothing but my bare hands and some crappy tools, I saved a kid's life. Brad couldn't take that away from me. Neither could Ai. My attention wandered to the office of this old gas station. With some work, it could make a cheap surgical suite good enough for DeeSeat. If I could get people to pay me something, I could get the right tools, maybe even hire a nurse.

"I don't suppose you could afford to pay me something? I'm kind of..." I groped for ways to fill in the blank that didn't seem pathetic or reveal too much. "Life is kind of beating me down right now."

Delusion wiped his knife on his jeans and stuck it in the sheath clipped to his belt. "I don't have anything, but Mom does. Come with us and you can ask her. She'll want to meet the guy who saved Phantom's life anyway."

Call me a bad person if you want, but hearing they had a mother surprised me. I'd figured them for street kids. "Sure," I said, still sitting on a cloud of invincibility. With a good night's sleep, a solid meal and a change of clothes, I could take on Ai in court, get the charges against me dropped, and have my license reinstated. I could do anything. Only the knowledge I looked like hell stopped me from marching home.

Five minutes later, I saw a black SUV stop on the cracked asphalt in front of the gas station. I hadn't been inside a road-rider in years. My car, a top-of-the-line sedan from only two years ago, accessed the city's paid grid and drove itself without touching the ground. Using the paid grid meant I soared over the schleps stuck in the public grid, or worse, the ground-bound grid.

Through the dingy, cracked glass, I watched two brawny men in trench coats like Delusion and Phantom's step out of the large vehicle and destroy my sense of victory. I could imagine each of them snapping me in half by glaring too hard. Delusion burst outside and ran to the one with the mohawk. He threw his arms around the man in the drizzle and held on for dear life.

Still inside, I gulped and checked Phantom's pulse again. No matter how heroic I might have been in Delusion's eyes, if this kid died, I had a strong feeling those two men wouldn't take it well.

CHAPTER 3

I picked up my suit jacket, smearing it with blood. Nothing could save it now, so I wiped my hands on it. Phantom still breathed and his heart still beat. My hands still shook too.

The door opened and a wall of man stepped through. His thick beard was enough to make me question my sanity for remaining in the room. Muscles bulged across his entire body and his mohawk stood in rain-wilted spikes. He clomped heavy black boots across the small room until he stood toe-to-toe with me. I had to look up to see his face.

"Delusion says you saved Phantom's life," he rumbled, his deep voice resonating in my chest.

My mouth went dry. At work, I always had the ability to call for security and the understanding that the doctor is the god in the room. No such barrier divided us here. This man radiated contained violence like a tiger paced inside him. An unbidden, unwanted visual of him punching his giant fist through my chest made me shiver. All thoughts of asking for payment fled.

"Yes," I squeaked. "He, ah, he still needs care." My voice cracked. I cleared my throat. "I did what I could here."

He stared at me, his dark eyes hard and flat. "Can you provide that care?"

"W-with the right tools and environment, yes." For the moment, I decided to be proud of myself for not wetting my pants and for only stuttering once.

His attention shifted to Phantom. "Get in the car," he spat at me.

"Yes, sir." I used extreme care to avoid touching him as I stepped around him. The moment my foot hit the asphalt outside, a voice inside my head screamed for me to run. Delusion had already climbed into the car. The other big man stood beside the open door, waiting for Phantom and the mohawk. They had no idea I'd been invited along.

I'd done my best for Phantom, but these people terrified me. Turning to flee, I saw the drab, gray street with its broken asphalt and scraggly weeds. Screens on the walls showed half-naked women and products I couldn't afford anymore. Flashing signs offered sex, drugs, and rock 'n roll without the glamor implied by the cliché. I had nothing to run to, only things to run from.

With a sigh, I hurried to the car and climbed inside. Delusion flashed me a grateful smile and clutched at my arm. Sitting on worn leather seats, we watched mohawk guy carry Phantom outside with more gentle care than I expected. Both big men climbed into the front seat, Phantom held in mohawk guy's lap, and the other guy started the engine.

Too nervous to speak, I gripped the plastic armrest and concentrated on breathing. We bounced over potholes and cracks. I saw crumbled buildings, desolate empty lots, a collapsed section of freeway, and blackened tree trunks stabbing the darkening sky. DeeSeat lived up to its name here, and I wondered how big a mistake I'd made by getting into this car.

"What kind of tools do you need to take care of Phantom?" mohawk guy asked.

I flinched, startled out of my thoughts. After a few moments of collecting my wits, I rattled off a list. At this point, Phantom needed a transfusion and stitches. Some internal work would speed his recovery, but he was young. He'd be better off without my stupid hands groping his kidney. "Whatever kind of pain medication you can get your hands on is a good idea," I said to finish of my list.

Thinking about what I'd done and seen with Phantom let me focus on something concrete that I understood. My grip on the armrest eased and I stopped waiting for the mohawk guy to whip around and slap me for daring to touch Phantom. I wished Delusion would let go of me so I couldn't be accused of anything untoward regarding him.

"I'm Hideo. May I know your name, please?"

Mohawk guy glanced back at me with a raised eyebrow. "Call me Monster. This is Wraith." he gestured to the driver.

I thought about commenting on the silly names. Wraith's huge paws on the steering wheel reminded me how easily I could be pummeled to death. He could probably do it by accident.

Manners, I heard my father's voice say in my head. *Never underestimate the power of good manners.* "Nice to meet you both."

Monster chuckled. "What're you doing in DeeSeat?"

The subtext of his question—why would someone like me be down here?—landed like a bag of bricks. Wraith pulled into a small, gravel parking lot while I thought about how to answer. We parked in a spot near the door of a long, low brick building painted black, with no markings besides the street number. Other old cars similar to ours sat in six of the ten spaces. Windows covered by dark curtains from the inside dotted the wall.

"Stumbling around," I finally said as we all stepped out of the vehicle. Delusion slid out behind me, still refusing to let go and trailing me like a lost puppy.

Wraith hurried to the black metal front door and opened it while Monster carried Phantom. "What do you want to be doing in DeeSeat, Hideo?" Monster asked as I followed him inside.

"I want to be a doctor again," I blurted.

Monster grunted. We plunged into a dim hallway with industrial carpet, bland, white walls, and faux wood doors marked with cheap plastic numbers. The place felt like a crappy apartment building or motel. Wraith stopped at door number nine and knocked. The hallway ended at door number ten.

The middle-aged woman who opened the door had dirty blonde hair held back by VR goggles perched on her head. Without the puckered scar cutting across the left side of her face and down her neck, she would've been a knockout.

My gaze dipped to her ample breasts, covered by skin-tight VR bodysuit. Ai had one, as did several of her friends. My colleagues and I didn't have time for that kind of crap. This woman's electric blue and black suit had several small, discolored patches. She could afford to have one, but not to repair it.

"Take him to his room." She stood aside to let Monster through, snapping my attention back to her face. The concern in her hazel eyes hadn't been echoed in her voice. Delusion dragged me inside.

"This is the doctor who saved his life," Delusion gushed. "Hideo."

We walked into a living room with an open kitchen and a hall leading deeper into the apartment. Her VR console projected a black circle with white crosshairs onto the dull beige carpet between two couches. Monster carried Phantom down the hall and out of sight.

"Is that so?" The woman bore a superficial resemblance to Delusion, mostly around her mouth and chin. She snatched my arm with a gloved hand, forcing me to stop only two steps inside.

I looked into her hard eyes and thought she could skin me if she didn't like my answer. "I did what I could. He still needs care. Monster has a shopping list."

She arched an eyebrow. "And who are you?"

"Doctor Hideo Tsukuda." I bowed to her like I'd trained myself to do with patients and their families. It was polite.

"Really." She snorted and her lips curled into a smirk. "You look more like a drunk."

I hadn't even noticed her checking me over. Heat flushed my cheeks. I never should've gone to that bar. Or the three before it. Not that things would be better. Probably, things would be worse. "It's...a long story."

Monster returned, headed for the door. "I'll be back with the doc's supplies in a few." With a tip of an imaginary hat, he hurried out. Wraith followed him, which felt like I'd been dismissed as a threat. I had no idea how to interpret that.

"Sit down, Dr. Tsukuda," the woman ordered. I complied without thinking. Ai had that effect on me too. So did my mother. "I see you follow instructions. That's good. Delusion, go sit with your brother."

I cleared my throat and summoned as much boldness as I could muster under the circumstances. "It would be good remove his wet clothes and wrap him in a blanket. Come get me if he develops a fever."

Delusion bobbed his head and dashed down the hall.

"So, Doctor Tsukuda, we have some time. Tell me your long story." She gave the impression of a spider in her web, trying to lure the fly closer.

I took a deep breath and hoped I didn't step in anything sticky.

CHAPTER 4

"The short version is my wife threw me out because she's an uptight bitch and my boss fired me because he's an asshole." I noticed my hands shaking again and laced my fingers in my lap to make them stop. "I'm sorry, I didn't hear your name?"

"Misery." She stepped into the kitchen and fetched a plastic cup from a cabinet.

"You all have unusual names here."

Misery laughed, the sound grating and harsh. "Don't you watch the holos, Dr. Tsukuda?"

"Not really. I work too much. My wife is a fan of some and prattles about them all the time. I can't say I've ever paid much attention."

She filled the cup with water from a pitcher in the fridge and brought it to me. "And she's an uptight bitch, right?" she mocked.

I scowled and took the cup, then checked it for dissolving drugs. "That's not the point."

"Sure." She dropped onto the couch across from me and kept smirking. "We use handles here. To protect ourselves from the cops and other authorities. If you plan to stick around in DeeSeat, you should consider using one too."

Without my implant, I saw little danger of people using my real name. The cops only came to DeeSeat to pick up bodies and rescue people who called for help. On the other hand, one less way for them to find me seemed wise. No trail of people mentioning Dr. Tsukuda meant less chances for the police to wind up at my door.

I bowed my head. "I honor your experience and expertise."

"You're way too polite for DeeSeat. The people here will eat you alive. But never mind that. You'll learn. About that story? I didn't ask for the short version."

So much for deflecting her. I sipped the water and groped for how to begin. "I lost a patient on the table." The weight of that single moment settled on my shoulders, heavy enough to bow my spine. The memory of spurting blood filled my vision. Red covered my white latex gloves in thick, gushing splashes.

"That's an even shorter version, Dr. Tsukuda."

Jolted to the present, I saw Misery smirking at me again. My father's words surged out of my mouth and I bowed to her again. "My apologies, madam. I don't think I'm able to discuss this presently."

"I got that impression, so let's talk about Phantom instead. What's my son's condition? Monster told me he seems like he'll be fine, but you're the doctor."

I fished the spent bullet out of my pocket and handed it to her. "He should be fine once he's stitched up, so long as the wound is kept clean. The biggest concern is infection." That wasn't strictly true, but in my experience, most patients and their families only wanted to know the thing most likely to happen. Detailing all the potential issues tended to distract or upset people. Besides, telling Misery—a woman who commanded the loyalty of Monster and Wraith, and who knew how many others—I'd dug around inside her son's kidney with grease-stained pliers and my own dirty fingers seemed excessively stupid.

She jabbed a finger at me. "Just so we're clear, if he dies, so do you."

I froze, certain I'd misheard her. "I beg your pardon?"

"It's called an incentive."

"That's…" My mouth went dry and hung open.

"How things work in DeeSeat," she finished for me. "I'll have a room made up for you." She leaned forward, snagged my left wrist, and slapped a strip of metal around it before I could resist.

A tiny red light winked on the black metal strip and I squealed as it heated enough to burn my flesh. "What did you do?" I shrieked, tugging my hand to get it out of her grip.

"You're my guest until I say you can leave." She let go with a smug smirk.

I fell against the couch, cradling my wrist against my chest. Poking at the band proved fruitless. The metal had fused to my flesh. "This was unnecessary," I gasped, still reeling from the pain.

"This is called insurance."

Surviving this woman and her gang had suddenly become much more complicated. "How does it work?"

Misery held up a black, oblong controller with only one button. It fit into the palm of her hand with her thumb resting over the silvery button. She pressed it. Agony jolted my arm, then my spine, making me scream and crumple to the floor. The torture ended only a second after it had begun but still left me panting on my hands and knees.

"That's how it works, Dr. Tsukuda. Don't give me a reason and I won't use it."

I'd discovered how she earned her name, at least. I sat up and rubbed my face. The red light taunted me. Searching for words to fling in her face, I came up with only two, and they disappointed me. "I understand."

"Glad to hear it."

Monster breezed back inside, saving me from this situation. He carried a bulging plastic bag. "Everything you asked for, Doc."

Eager to be away from Misery, I stood and bowed to her. Without a word, I took the bag and almost fell over from the weight.

Taking it back, Monster chuckled. "I'll carry it, Doc."

Still unable to come up with anything to say, I fled for the hallway. Four crappy plastic doors stood open, and I poked my head into a beige and green bathroom before turning to see Monster pointing into Phantom's bedroom.

In my daughter's room, screens covered the walls. She interacted with them through her implant and by touch. Miko favored bright colors, balloons, and friendly animals. Soft fiber optic filaments made up her carpet so she could change the color whenever she wanted. Smooth, rounded corners and soft, plush toys surrounded her.

Phantom's room felt like someone had made an effort to be Miko's exact opposite. With all the sharp edges and open knife worship, I wondered how Phantom didn't stab himself routinely. Dark curtains blocked all but a sliver of the harsh streetlight outside. Delusion's coat lay in a crumpled heap on the bland carpet.

"Delusion," Monster barked from behind me, making me jump. "Go to your mom. Now."

I skittered inside as the boy stood from his brother's bedside. "It wasn't our fault," Delusion whined.

"I don't care." Monster set his meaty hand on the top of Delusion's head and used it to shove him into the hallway. "Tell her." He watched with a stern scowl while Delusion slumped his shoulders and shuffled away. "Do you need an assistant, Doc?"

The dynamics of this family didn't concern me. So long as Misery didn't beat her boys, her approach to discipline was none of my business. They had concerns I didn't understand, and teaching them how to handle a rough life seemed like a valuable lesson. If I told myself this enough times, I could forget about the leash on my wrist.

"Are these your sons?" I can't explain what made me

ask. Neither boy resembled Monster in any way, and Misery hadn't behaved like a lover toward him. The arrangement here seemed important for my survival, I suppose.

Monster smirked at me. "Not in the way you mean. Their father is dead. I watch out for them, though, so kind of, yeah."

Nodding, I unbuttoned my shirt sleeves and rolled them up. "I could use another pair of hands, yes. You don't mind the sight of blood, I hope?"

He laugh as he knelt and emptied the shopping bag. "I'm fine, Doc. I see you're going to be our guest. I'll find some clothes in your size."

"Thank you." Picking up a box of latex gloves bolstered my confidence in this strange place.

"What's this for?" Monster held up a plastic shower curtain liner in an unopened package.

"Open it up and we'll get it under Phantom. To protect him from the bed and the bed from him."

Monster chuckled. "We have tarps big enough for that."

I wondered if he knew that because they often wrapped up dead bodies. "This one is as sterile as something like that can be."

He grunted and ripped the package open. I used more restraint to open the box in my hands and snapped on latex gloves. Setting the box aside, I peered at everything else he'd bought for me. A small vial of clear liquid caught my eye and I crouched to pick it up. Reading the label sent my brow climbing up my forehead.

"Where did you get morphine?" My hospital hadn't used morphine in at least two decades. They'd been phasing it out of texts when I started medical school. I didn't even know someone still made and packaged it.

"Corner drugstore." Monster picked Phantom up and I rushed to arrange the shower curtain under him.

"You're joking. Right?"

"No, probably just using the term differently than you do." He set Phantom down so I had easy access to his injury.

I pictured a boarded-up building with a hidden entrance in the back and a hunched old man tending dozens of shelves of drugs. A single, old fashioned light bulb dangled bare in the center and he used a hand-held flashlight to check the labels. This man muttered to himself for some reason.

"Are you sure this is what it says?"

"I asked my guy for a high-caliber painkiller. That

bottle is what he gave me. He doesn't fuck around with me, if that's what you're worried about. It might not actually be what it says, but it's not poison or anything."

The bottle had an intact seal, and the date stamped on the side—marking it as expired twelve years ago—had what looked like a proper lot number. With no discoloration in the liquid, I felt confident it wouldn't harm Phantom. Whether it had enough efficacy left to help was questionable, but it would be better than nothing. With no injector gun in sight, I found a sterile syringe and used it to inject Phantom with what I estimated to be a proper dose of the drug.

"You want me to rip off this tape?"

I had a feeling Monster subscribed to the tough-it-out school of recovery. Unfortunately, his idea would probably be enough additional trauma to send Phantom into shock. "Give the drug a few minutes first." Snapping the cap over the syringe, I dropped it into the now-empty bag and arranged the supplies on Phantom's bedside table.

"Are you going to toss that needle?"

"Yes, of course. It's used." Though I hadn't used a syringe more than a few times since medical school, I knew that much.

"I'll take care of it."

For a moment, I thought nothing of Monster's statement. Then I noticed him pluck the needle out of the bag and turn to leave. He also picked up the half-full bottle of morphine.

I gulped, afraid of the answer, but had to ask anyway. "Where are you taking that?"

"Not your concern, Doc. I'll be back in a few." He left too fast for me to stop him.

"Sterilize the needle!" I called after him.

CHAPTER 5

By the time Monster returned, I had the duct tape pried off Phantom's skin. Lucky for him, it hadn't stuck well and only a few spots needed care in removal. I did my best to ignore Monster as anything other than an assistant while I cleaned the wound with rubbing alcohol and stitched it shut. My hands shook anyway.

"I thought all you fancy doctors had rock-steady hands," Monster said as I tied off the last stitch. He traded me a pair of scissors for the needle.

Taking a deep breath, I steadied myself before cutting the thread. "I apologize for being nervous under your scrutiny."

Monster chuckled. "Don't worry, Doc. You're part of the family now."

"I already have a family." Except I didn't. I set the scissors aside and taped gauze over the wound site. All business. No feelings. "This bandage needs to be kept on and dry for the next twenty-four hours. After that—"

"You can tell him tomorrow," Monster said, waving me off. He wrestled with his latex gloves while I peeled mine off with ease. "I'll show you to your room now, unless you'd rather have dinner with us."

Frowning at his interruption, I wondered if I had the option to eat by myself. I decided not to ask. Until I knew these people better, I had no idea what would annoy them. They all struck me as people not to annoy. "Dinner would be appreciated."

We picked up all the supplies together and rolled Phantom off the shower curtain. Monster wrapped him in a clean blanket and shooed me out of the room.

"Doc," he said as he shut Phantom's door. "What's your 'link code?"

I rattled it off without thinking and immediately regretted it. "It doesn't work, though." When Monster raised an eyebrow at me, I sighed. "My implant was disabled."

"How interesting," Misery said. She sat on the couch in the living room with a glass goblet of dark liquid, now wearing a blue shirt and jeans. "That makes you fairly useless, doesn't it? I don't even know where to get a handheld 'link, and I can get my hands on a carburetor for a '67 Chevy."

Somehow, I doubted things labeled "useless" survived for long around her. I bowed to her, scrambling for some way to justify myself lest she decide to jolt me again. "It wasn't damaged or removed, only disabled. I'm sure it can be switched on again, I just don't know anyone who can do that."

"And you can't pay for it." She sipped at her drink, watching me over the rim of her glass with a pointed, unfriendly stare.

"No, madam, I can't." My mind whirled with the possibilities if I could get it back in operation. Though these people terrified me, they'd claimed me. I had no other options and hoped that saving Phantom had earned me enough goodwill to be able to make mistakes without punishment. I swallowed my fear and plunged headfirst into what I hoped wouldn't be a disaster. "Perhaps we can come to some sort of arrangement?"

"Perhaps we can, Dr. Tsukuda." Misery eyed me with enough intensity to suspect she could see through my flesh. "I'll think about it. Monster, take him to his room."

Monster clamped a paw on my shoulder and pushed me to the front door. I didn't resist. Apparently, I wouldn't be a guest for dinner after all. We stepped into the hallway and he shoved me at door number eight, directly across the hall. Opening it, I stepped into the kitchen of a much smaller apartment than Misery's. The kitchen had a nook with a twin bed and a door leading to a tiny bathroom. Thin, brown curtains covered the single window over the bed and the ceiling had one frosted plastic light fixture.

"Someone will bring some clothes later." Monster tossed a key at me, which I failed to catch. It clattered on the plastic flooring. "There's food in the cabinet. Whenever you need to check on Phantom, just knock." He shut the door before I came up with a response.

I crouched and picked up the key, running my fingers over the floor. The blank, hard surface reminded me of my first date with Ai. Our mothers had set us up on a blind date and paid for a nice dinner at a nice restaurant. Afterward, we had tickets to a play, but neither of us wanted to see it. As we walked around with no particular destination in mind, we passed a crappy little cafe with blank plastic flooring and a synth musician playing in the corner. I danced with her and decided I could live with her as my wife.

Straightening, I wished I could go back and tell that moron never to see her again. I set the key on the marbled plastic counter and opened each of four cabinets. Monster's idea of "food" consisted of three dozen cans of the tasteless mush only the poorest people eat. Since Ai kicked me out, I'd managed to avoid this shit. Until now.

The label called it *PROCESSED FOOD PRODUCT*. Several cans claimed to have flavors. I didn't trust any of them. Some soulless company made it out of "actual animal parts," plus vitamins, minerals, unspecified grains, and the tears of cuisine chefs.

In the fridge, I found ketchup, mustard, and mayonnaise. Why on earth anyone would want those with Processed Food Product mystified me. I turned the kitchen upside-down until I found salt, pepper and sugar. Resigned to my fate, I grabbed a random can and pulled the tab. The smell made me reconsider, but I hadn't eaten since yesterday. On reflection, I probably shouldn't have had so much whiskey. My tolerance for it amazed me.

I dumped some salt into the can, swirled around the gruel-like slop, and sipped it. Salt-flavored oatmeal tasted better than this. Unbidden, thoughts of grilled salmon with a lemon rub came to mind. The night before everything went to shit, I took Ai and Miko out to dinner at our favorite restaurant. Ai had her favorite meal, fresh unagi. Miko played with tempura shrimp more than she ate it. Staring into my can of beige pig slop, the smells of those foods mingling together in my memory finally cracked me.

My eyes burned and I wanted to scream. For the past three days, I'd shuffled from place to place in a haze of denial. I'd kicked a garbage can over on my way out of the hospital. Nothing else had registered until now, except in a detached, clinical way.

Ai never liked that about me. I didn't emote enough for her. She crumbled into tears at chick flicks and birthday parties while I stood by, stoic and unmoved. I'll never forget the one time I sat on the couch with Miko, reading her a stupid little story. Ai watched us and burst into tears. Later, she said it reminded her of the man she married, whatever that meant. I hadn't changed much since we met.

I slid to the floor and leaned against the cabinet with tears sliding down my cheeks. This happened. One mistake destroyed my life. Brad said I was drunk, but I wasn't. Two hours before surgery, I'd downed one shot. Or two? Maybe it had been two. Ai had thrown me out the day before, so I could hardly be blamed for dipping into my work stash to take the edge off.

At least I'd been able to leave the hospital before the

police arrived. Fishing in my pocket, I found the last of my paper money. If Misery or Monster found it, I suspected they'd take it. Not that such a small amount of cash would get me far.

Wiping my face, I clambered to my feet and stuffed the money into the drawer with a scattering of plastic utensils. If they looked, they'd find it. I picked up the key and stared at it, wondering who had copies. Who could come in and slit my throat in my sleep?

I dropped it onto the counter again and forced myself to drink my shit in a can.

CHAPTER 6

"You should empty that entire bottle by lunchtime," I told Phantom the next morning. So far, I'd choked down one entire can of Processed Food Product. Phantom got to drink strawberry-flavored protein shakes, which seemed acceptable to cover the liquids he needed. "Call for help to empty your bladder so you don't rip your stitches. We'll use this bedpan until you can walk safely."

"Gross," Phantom breathed. He still lay on his bed, wiped out by the act of letting me check his temperature and blood pressure. Dark circles under his eyes and pale cheeks told me he'd be in that bed for a while.

The corner of my mouth ticked up. Administering to a patient put me on solid ground. Monster and Wraith not being here helped. I even had clean clothes now, and had been able to take a shower and shave. "Nurses usually handle that, so I'm right there with you. Here's hoping you can get up soon, but don't push it too hard. For now, get some sleep."

"Thanks, Doc Soo," he mumbled.

I nodded and backed out, leaving the door open so he could be heard. Delusion hunched on a couch in the living room, chewing on his fingernails. His right foot bounced.

"He's going to be fine," I assured Delusion. "I'm not just saying that."

"That's what Monster said."

His jittery nerves made me nervous too. I snapped off my latex gloves and tossed them in the kitchen garbage. "Where is everyone?"

"Out."

"Will they be back soon?"

Delusion flinched and shook his head. "I dunno." Their kitchen had a black coffeemaker, among other things. I had a feeling I was lucky to have a refrigerator in mine.

A bang in the hallway made us both flinch. Delusion jumped to his feet and fled for his room. Uncertainty gripped me. I took two steps toward Phantom's room before Monster tossed the front door open. His gaze locked onto mine.

"Doc, come with me." The grim set of his jaw drew my feet like a dark magnet that didn't want to be whipped or zapped for disobedience. He led me to door number ten.

Instead of another apartment, we entered a small room with nothing but a metal chair bolted to the plascrete floor. It had no windows, no carpet, no decoration, and nothing else but a paper shopping bag and a bare lightbulb screwed into a metal housing in the plascrete ceiling.

Misery watched while Wraith wrestled a new man into the chair. Monster stepped to his side and used plastic straps at his wrists, ankles, and neck to keep him in place. An extra band wrapped around the man's chest.

Blood flecked the man's mouth and nose, and a black eye ripened under shaggy, dark hair as I watched. He wore a dirty, blood-speckled tank top and shiny black pants with no shoes or socks. As soon as he was secure, Monster dragged me inside and shut the door. I gulped, not sure what to think of my presence here. Without missing a beat, Monster turned, took three swift steps, and punched the restrained man in the face. I jumped and backed into the wall with a squeak. The restrained man grunted.

"Doc, c'mere," Monster said without looking at me.

Horrified, I slid along the wall to reach the doorknob. "Why?"

Misery snorted and stepped into my path. "Doc,

meet Deadbolt."

Deadbolt spat blood to the side and grunted again. Monster had broken his nose and he only grunted with mild discomfort. Fresh fear rolled over me in a tsunami. Too many dangerous men filled this room. And Misery.

"Why am I here?" I asked, unable to raise my voice above a whisper.

Monster stood aside and jabbed a finger at Deadbolt. "Fix his nose."

The moment felt surreal. Monster had brought me here to align a nose he hadn't yet broken, presumably knowing he intended to do so. I wanted to ask why, to refuse, to run screaming from the room. All these things could, I suspected, get me beaten or killed. I gulped and approached the man. Straightening broken noses had been part of my job back when I worked in the ER as a resident.

"Th-this will hurt." My voice cracked. I didn't repeat myself. Placing my hands on his face, I took a deep breath. With a quick jerk, I wrenched the cartilage back into alignment. Deadbolt grunted again, this time with genuine pain.

"Good job, Doc." Monster held up Deadbolt's head by the chin.

I backed away again. "May I go now?"

"No," Misery snapped with a dark grin. "You're going to stay here and keep Deadbolt going as long as possible. Supplies are in the bag." She pointed to the paper bag.

Her orders took until Monster punched Deadbolt in the gut to sink in. I wanted to throw up. "N-no." I retreated to the corner, unable to tear my gaze away from Monster hitting Deadbolt again and again. "No, I won't do that. I won't help you torture him."

Misery rushed me. She grabbed my shirt and pointed a gun at my forehead. I hadn't seen a gun this close before and had no idea where she'd been hiding it. My heart stopped beating and I stopped breathing.

"I gather I was unclear last night, so let me fix that now, Doctor." Glaring at me, she leaned in until only an inch separated our noses.

Thankfully, I had used the bathroom recently. Otherwise, I would've wet my new jeans as I cringed away from her. My mind replayed all the stupidest mistakes I'd ever made. Fucking a patient's wife in my office rose to the top of the list. Bunny had everything in all the right places. She'd fawned over me. Only now, staring death in the face, did I realize how much of a moron I'd been to piss away my decent marriage and only child for large breasts.

"Your entire job while you're here is to do whatever I tell you to." Misery's steely voice snapped me back to the present. "I'm happy you saved Phantom's life. That really does make me happy. You have kids, Doctor?" When I nodded, she smiled. It didn't reach her eyes. "Then you understand that part. The problem is, if I let you walk away, some other gang will find you and snap you up. Someone with your skills is a commodity. That's why you have the wristband.

"So, you work for me now. I give you a place to stay and food to eat. I'll find someone to re-activate your implant and pay them. You," she shoved my forehead with the gun barrel, "do what I tell you to. I'm telling you to do whatever it takes to keep this man alive as long as possible. When he dies, he better be such a fucking mess that I don't suspect you gave him a mercy killing. Are we clear, or do I need to get the button out?"

"Yes," I whimpered. "Clear." What other answer could I give? When she withdrew the gun, I slid to the floor and remembered to breathe. I'd fallen into the deep end of a pool I didn't understand and had no idea what to do about it.

Monster slammed his fist into Deadbolt's flesh over and over with meaty thwacks. I'd smelled blood a thousand times in a surgical suite, but the copper in the air here turned my stomach. Squeezing my eyes shut against the beating, I wished I could block out sounds. Monster reached a point where he growled with the effort of pounding on this man. At that point, Deadbolt could only whimper.

After far too long, the sounds changed to panting and wheezing. I opened my eyes to see Deadbolt's head hanging forward, blood drooling out of his mouth. Monster stood back, wiping his fist with a towel. Misery stepped forward and grabbed Deadbolt by the hair. She inspected his face, looking him over critically. With a huff of disgust, she let go.

"Dammit, Monster, he's unconscious. You were supposed to stop before that."

"Sorry." Monster didn't sound sorry. "Got carried away, I guess."

Wraith chuckled. He appeared to have no other purpose in the room than watching the proceeds. Deadbolt couldn't escape. Maybe he'd take the next beating shift.

Misery turned to me. "Wake him up and fix whatever you can."

"Are you going to kill him?" The question burbled

out of me against my will.

Misery raised her brow. "You probably don't want to ask that."

"No, I don't," I forced myself to say as I crawled to the bag of supplies and pawed through it. Somehow, though, I felt I had to justify the question. "Just need to decide how to prioritize the injuries."

"How practical." Misery smirked. "He'll die, but not yet. We still have some questions to ask him. You don't shoot one of my boys and walk away."

I swallowed bile. "I see." Without looking at her, Monster, or Wraith, I dragged the bag to Deadbolt's side and snapped latex gloves on. My initial examination told me he'd sustained mostly superficial injuries. When I prodded his sixth left rib, he winced, but it didn't shift, so I suspected it was cracked.

"Ah, not out cold after all," Misery cooed. "Go ahead, Doc. Clean him up and put on bandages."

Already using a wet wipe on his face, I bit back a rude retort that I didn't need to be told how to do my job. Instead, I took a deep breath and tried to see Deadbolt as a practice patient. "That seems like a waste of bandages."

Misery and her two flunkies laughed. "I suppose it

is," she said. "You're living up to your reputation, Doc."

I froze. "What?"

Misery crouched beside me with a grin. "You were so nice to give me your full name, Dr. Hideo Tsukuda. I looked you up. Seems your face is plastered all over the 'net and the holonews. Murdered a patient, cheated on your wife with the dead guy's wife, and an alcoholic. You're a regular piece of shit, aren't you? Did you beat your wife? How about your kid?"

"No!" Heat flared in my cheeks. I wanted to crawl into a hole and die. My mind flashed to the surgical suite three days ago.

Standing over Arthur Belton's prone body covered with blue sheeting, I looked down at the open incision. Gabby controlled suction. Marissa handed tools to me. Paula assisted. Blood covered my gloves. I directed the nanites to devour the aging man's disintegrating hip while I held his pelvis in place and cut the ends off his ligaments. I saw his iliac artery. My fingers twitched and I sliced the artery in half.

I don't know why.

That was a lie. I knew exactly why. As I stared, I remembered Bunny telling me how much she hated being married to a decrepit old man. She wanted to feel like a woman again, so she said. Someone so skilled with his hands could do the job. Then she unzipped my pants and gave me a blow job in my office.

None of this would've happened without that blow job.

CHAPTER 7

I threw up into the toilet in my room. Deadbolt had, at most, an hour left to live. I'd done my job in silence for five hours—taping cuts, straightening bones, breaking smelling salts, and cleaning abrasions. Nothing in Misery's bag provided any kind of anesthetic, and she'd gotten the most caustic cleaning agents possible.

Deadbolt's screams still echoed in my ears. My ministrations had proven the more horrific part of his session, a fact that bothered me more than anything else I saw in that room. Monster and Wraith took turns punching, slapping, kicking, and even cutting Deadbolt. He endured it all with little reaction. Then I swooped in.

I may have killed Arthur Belton, but he felt nothing. He went under sedation and never woke up. Besides, doctors made mistakes all the time. No one liked to admit it, but Belton was far from the first patient I'd lost on the table.

Processed Food Product looked and tasted about the same coming up as going down. I flushed the toilet and shambled to the kitchen sink. Cool water felt good on my face and cleared the bile from my mouth and sinuses. Leaning over it, I squeezed my eyes shut against the too-fresh memory of Deadbolt.

Getting my implant re-activated was worth this. Right? With it I could steady my hands and keep myself under control. I'd be more useful and could negotiate for better conditions, maybe even bargain to get this stupid wristband off and leave. That abandoned gas station could be converted to a medical suite. I could take patients and avoid the cops. With the right DeeSeat contacts, I could run an underground body shop.

That meant doing whatever Misery wanted until I could make my own way. She'd protect me from guys like Deadbolt. I couldn't say if she'd protect me from her own people, but if I patched them up enough times, they'd respect me as the doctor in the house. I could set limits and refuse to help with torture.

"Hideo, you're fucked," I muttered. Wishing I had a bottle of whiskey, I staggered to my bed and dropped onto it. The textured ceiling had a dark boot print I hadn't noticed last night or this morning. How it got there, a mystery I had no frame of reference to understand, crowded everything else out of my mind. Briefly.

The boot print reminded me of Monster's boots, which brought me back to the horrors of room ten. I rubbed my eyes and urged myself to look at the episode from Misery's perspective. She had to punish anyone who attacked her people or her gang would be perceived as weak. Without my intervention, Phantom probably would have died, which meant her retaliation needed to be rapid and devastating.

I hadn't paid much attention to the questions and answers in room ten. My sanity had depended upon keeping my eyes averted and memories of Miko close at hand. To save myself now, I remembered her fourth birthday party.

Ai made her wear a blue silk dress with embroidered gold dragons. I thought the dress an extravagant waste, but Ai insisted on something special for her last birthday before kindergarten. When Ai presented Miko with her dark hair in silky ribbons and wearing that dress, Miko bit her lip and looked at the floor. I switched off my emotion regulator and felt an almost unbearable swell of paternal love for my sweet little girl.

"I thought you said you were bringing Miko," I told

Ai, putting a trace of confusion in my voice. "I only see Amaterasu in the flesh before me."

Miko's small face lit up with joy. I scooped her into my arms and hugged her. She wrapped her arms around my neck and kissed my cheek.

Ai ripped her out of my arms and jabbed a sharp, red fingernail in my face. "You lying, cheating bastard," she snarled. I'd never seen her so angry and took a step back.

"I didn't mean to," I protested.

She slapped me. "Your dick *accidentally* fell into that whore?"

Rubbing my cheek, I scrambled to find words to fix this. "It wasn't my fault. I can only resist so much—"

She slapped me again. "Bullshit, Hideo. You saw something you wanted and you took it. Just like you always do. Get out. If you try to get custody of Miko, I will bury you in an avalanche."

My eyes snapped open in filtered sunlight. Someone pounded on my door, probably for the second or third time. I lurched off the bed and hurried to the door as fast as my sleep-fogged brain would let me.

"Doc, open the fucking door!"

I wrenched the door open to find Monster in the act

of reaching up to knock again. "Sorry," I mumbled. "Passed out."

"Get your ass moving, Doc."

"What do you need now?" I shut the door and followed him, choosing not to go back in for the key. If someone snuck in, they were welcome to the Processed Food Product.

"Ungrateful son of a bitch," Monster spat.

"I don't understand?"

Monster clamped a hand on my shoulder and half-dragged me to room ten—already spotless—without another word. He tossed me inside and shut the door, leaving me alone with the chair and a new person. I couldn't determine their gender by looking. They wore a grease-stained welding apron over baggy cargo pants with bulging pockets and a loose, button-down shirt. A brown trench coat obscured most of their frame. Dark-lensed goggles hid their eyes and neither the round jaw nor the short, brown hair offered any good hints.

This person perched on the arm of the chair and looked up from tapping on a tablet. "You must be Doc?" Their voice sounded like a husky alto to me. I decided it must be a woman.

"Yes."

"That's kinda generic. You may want to add something to it, like Doctor Death or Doc Martin. Doc Brown. Something."

"Thank you for the suggestion." I had no idea what else to say. Trapped in room ten with a strange woman left me uncertain of my situation.

She cracked a grin and hopped to her booted feet. "They said you were polite. I like that. So many assholes in this world." Flashing me a bright smile, she patted the back of the chair. "Have a seat, Doc."

I gulped. "Why?"

Her goggles moved like her brow raised. "So I can reach the back of your head? You're what, five foot ten? That's six inches taller than me."

"Are you going to strap me down?"

"Only if you want me to, Doc. I can make this kinky if it'll help you relax."

For several seconds, I stared at her. "I don't understand. Who are you?"

She laughed. "Your friendly neighborhood implant hacker. Call me Splice."

"Implant—?" My mind reeled. Had I missed

something? Did I perform so well in here before that Misery decided to reward me already? "You're here to re-activate my implant?"

"Yep." Splice patted the chair again. "Take a load off."

I turned away from the chair and sat cross-legged on the floor. Maybe these people weren't as awful as they seemed. They'd given the impression I'd be an indentured slave for months or years before they had my implant taken care of. And then I'd still be a slave. I rubbed my wristband and wondered if she could remove it. Since Monster left me alone with her, she probably couldn't. Either that, or she wouldn't due to some arrangement with the gang.

"When did they contact you for this?"

"A few hours ago. Do you happen to know which protocol was used to disable?"

Without knowing the time, I couldn't guess how long ago they'd finished with Deadbolt. I did know the sun hadn't gone down yet. Thinking about time made my stomach rumble.

"I'll take that as a no and get to work here, Doc. Sit still and think of England."

"What? Why? Is history important to this?"

She knelt behind me and pressed a cold metal wand

to the flesh behind my ear. "No. It's just a saying. It means relax and pretend you're enjoying this."

"Will it hurt?"

"Nope, it'll just feel weird."

Closing my eyes, I took calming breaths and tried not to fidget. Everything would be fine when Splice finished. I'd be able to connect to the 'net, and that would solve all my problems.

Some of my problems.

One problem. It would solve exactly one problem.

With that realization, I sighed. "I'm still fucked," I muttered.

"Welcome to the Darkside," Splice murmured. She shoved a heated needle into my neck.

CHAPTER 8

My world expanded in an instant. My 'link connected to the internet and I saw the data streams all around me. They ran everywhere, though thinner than I was used to. By reflex, I accessed my account and let it feed me the time and date, the weather, my curated news feed, and notifications, all as an overlay on my vision. The world righted itself. I felt like I'd regained a missing limb.

"By the sound of that happy sigh, I'm going to declare success." Splice wiped behind my ear with rough gauze and patted me on the back.

Flicking through my messages, I saw several from Ai with a subject line of "divorce." I ignored them.

"So you know, when your implant was disabled, your GPS tracker wasn't. The fact you've avoided the police until now is entirely because you came to DeeSeat where GPS doesn't work very well. I've disabled it. My advice would be not to use your personal account, because the temptation to do or say something stupid is really high, and it's possible for the police to hijack you through it even without the GPS."

With another sigh, this one much less pleased, I hung my head. "Tell me what to do."

She set a hand on my shoulder and squeezed gently. "You're going to be okay. This isn't the end of the world, it's just the end of a phase in your life." With another squeeze, she gave me a sympathetic smile. "Access your account manager, wipe all your personal data. Save it. Ignore all the dire warnings and keep pressing it to save until it does. Then archive the account manager. You'll have to relearn how to use your implant interface, but we've all been there, done that. It's like a rite of passage in DeeSeat."

"I'll lose everything." While I had no problems with never accessing Ai's angry messages, I kept pics of Miko and had access to my— "I should empty my bank account first."

Splice blinked, then shook her head. "Unless you already have a secondary bank account set up, you'd have to authenticate to do that. Even if it's a really small amount, that'll send up a flashing beacon pointing straight at you. I said the cops leave most people most alone in DeeSeat. When you infringe on the regular world, they toss that out the window and bring in High Threat Response teams to splatter your brains on the pavement."

Disappointment must have shown on my face, because she added, "That life is gone, Doc. All of it. You're starting over from scratch."

"Great." Damn Bunny for fucking my life with that blow job. "I have a daughter."

"No, you don't. You have a blank slate. Whatever brought you down here, she's better off thinking you're dead."

Her words punched me in the chest. "I can't. She's only—"

"Yeah, you can. The other choice is you try to see her and the cops arrest you. Stay around here and you're safe. Leave and you're in jail. Trust me when I say your daughter will be better off thinking you escaped or died than seeing you in the hellhole that is the Auburn Incarceration Facility." Her expression hardened and darkened. "AIF isn't a place you want her to ever have to visit."

I remembered Miko in a series of flashes—twirling in her fairy princess tutu, as a baby in my arms, throwing spaghetti everywhere, smashing cake into her face, gazing up at me with uncomplicated love. My memories would torment me for the rest of my life. I'd never see her do so many things.

Pressing my lips together to keep a scream of anguish bottled inside, I stood and bowed to Splice. "Thank you for your help. I appreciate it. If you're ever injured, I'm a surgeon and will gladly help you."

"That so? Huh. Misery didn't mention that tiny fact." She stood and brushed her hands over her pants. Though I had many other things on my mind, her gesture drew my attention to her crotch. The fabric bunched there, leading me to wonder if I'd guessed her gender wrong. "You know how to attach and implant cybernetics?"

I nodded and remembered everything my implant allowed me to do. My emotions didn't have to rule me anymore. Activating the regulator drew the poison out of the wound. Leaving myself that way would erode my sanity, but I could maintain my composure for Splice's benefit. "My specialty is tissue and bone replacement. I'm accustomed to working with a full nanosuite, but learned originally without."

"That's kinda interesting to me, because my business includes building cybernetic body part replacements and enhancements." She stood and we shook hands, then she told me her 'link code. "We should talk more about this."

"I'd like that. Thank you." Though it seemed I should leave, I rubbed the wristband. "I'm not sure how to ask this."

She smirked. "If I could remove that thing in five minutes, I'd do it, Doc. I do know the guy who builds them for Misery, but I don't have the schematics. Without that, it'd take me a few hours with equipment I don't have here to be sure I can remove it."

Monster had made a grave mistake in putting me in that room alone with Splice. Finding a way out of here without oversight couldn't be impossible. No matter how many people their gang had here, a moment would arise when I could slip out. My room even had a window.

"Thank you. That gives me...things to think about."

"Yeah, me too." Splice opened the door and I followed her out.

Returning to room eight, I initiated the data removal Splice had instructed me to take care of. A flick of my will brought up my account information. Forty-one years ago, Doctor Soren Elstermann entered my Citizen Identification Number, birthdate, and parents' names. Before my fifth birthday, my father had populated most of the rest of the fields. On my eighteenth birthday, the password he'd locked it with expired.

For twenty-three years, I'd dutifully updated the account, just like everyone else. Deleting my CIN felt like treason. The twelve-digit number vanished one character at a time. I watched it happen, thinking someone would break down the door any moment to arrest me for having the audacity to modify indelible account information.

My birthdate disappeared next, then my mother's name and my father's name. Numerous other fields went blank, one by one. All my certifications disappeared. I sat on my bed, holding my head. Activating the save feature took all my willpower.

Up popped a message.

Are you sure you wish to delete your account data?

I took a deep breath and confirmed.

Deleting this information is illegal under West America law. Delete anyway?

Yes.

If you continue, you cannot recover this information without a paid governmental records search. Continue or Cancel?

Continue.

Proceeding with this action will cause a beacon to be

activated, notifying police of your location and activities. Proceed or Cancel?

This message gave me pause. Splice said she'd deactivated my GPS. What if she didn't know about some other beacon? Then again, she'd obviously done it herself and said to ignore all the scary messages. At this point, the process seemed more annoying than frightening anyway. A lesser man might give up the fight as too big a pain in the ass. I took another deep breath and continued through that message, and the next seven.

Finally, the messages stopped and it deleted everything. I stared at the blank form, not sure what would happen now. The freedom I'd gained felt elusive and distant. Of course, it also limited me—no one without an account could move freely in West America. If I wanted to leave DeeSeat, I had to enter fake information into my account manager and hope no one noticed. There might be ways to get to Portland's Undercity or San Francisco's Downland, but I expected crossing the space between would take a lot of effort and a lot of money.

Bunny had shoved me into a little box, that bitch. I rubbed my face and remembered I'd activated my emotion regulator. Part of me wanted to leave it running. The rest of me understood the complex chemical reactions in my brain it interfered with. Over time, it would destroy my ability to deal with even the most innocuous emotion.

With a start, I realized that had happened. Since I shambled out of my daze yesterday, every little thing had either set me off or shut me down. I'd been bouncing from one overload to another, barely able to keep my shit together. For years, the thing had been running almost nonstop. It made me cool, rational, and logical.

So cool, rational, and logical that I killed a man without a second thought.

I switched it off.

CHAPTER 9

Two days passed with nothing more challenging than Phantom's stitches. No infection had yet to rear its ugly head and no one else needed my skills, either for good or ill. This left me with far too much time to think. I thought about how I'd never see Miko again. Finding someone else to have a child with might fill that hole. Someday. Maybe.

Everything else, I sidestepped. I'm a coward, I guess. The chain of events that started two weeks ago made me cycle through emotions so fast I could hardly understand them. Bunny inspired rage-filled hate and lustful longing at the same time. Memories of Ai and Miko made me despair for the pleasant life that slipped through my fingers. And then there was Brad.

Looking back, I had to admit that even though Brad had been the one to fire me and deactivate my implant, he'd also given me a chance to flee. He could have called security and had me escorted into police custody. He could have locked me in my office. He could have dosed me into unconsciousness. Instead, he'd breezed in, announced my fate, stabbed me behind the ear, and breezed out again.

I owed him. Despite his part in imploding my life, he'd given me a chance to escape when he didn't need to. His actions made no sense to me, though I suppose we'd been friends. We went out drinking together sometimes. We complained about our wives to each other. We worked together on complicated, high-profile patients. That didn't seem like enough.

Setting the mystery of Brad aside yet again, I considered what I'd learned last night. I'd had dinner with Misery, Delusion, and Phantom, which had involved pretend food one step up in quality compared to those awful cans of gruel. The meat's flavor had mimicked chicken, sort of. I could almost believe the vegetables had been grown someplace. Almost.

From what I understood of the light conversation, Misery served as the leader for a street gang calling itself Nightmares. The name struck me as melodramatic and silly, but all their fake names fit the theme, more or less. They controlled territory and moved drugs in some fashion involving delivery to users. If I wanted the latest street drug, I only had to ask. I'd be lying if I said I wasn't tempted. Misery told me about something called Memless, which fucks your brain up so hard you get amnesia for a day. Not having to deal with my memories of Miko...

Were it not for my understanding of how amnesia can become permanent, I might have tried it. But I'd spent too many years of my life gaining medical expertise and experience to take that kind of chance. She understood. I also refrained from asking for a bottle of whiskey for unknown reasons.

I dumped my brand-new cereal—Misery's idea of a reward for staying after my implant activation—into a bowl and poured sugar and synthetic milk over it. This stuff tasted about the same as Processed Food Product with the marginal improvement of being crunchy. The sugar made it edible.

Why hadn't I asked for alcohol? I still puzzled at that. There had been a bottle in my desk for years. Most days, I had a drink when I got home. Whiskey took the edges off for me. Considering my situation, a stiff drink seemed like a no-brainer. Then again, I did need to keep my wits close at hand if I wanted to find a way out. Alcohol would probably make that a challenge.

As I picked up my spoon, my 'link flashed with a message from Splice. I shoveled cereal into my mouth while I sent the command to open the message. It scrolled across my vision.

[Splice: Can you sneak out tonight? I've got a customer buying a spinal upgrade implant who needs a surgeon to put it in properly. She can pay and I know she's good for it. If you can do it tonight, I can set it up for you. Otherwise, she can get a guy tomorrow.]

Blinking rapidly at this unexpected good fortune, my mind raced through all the logistical concerns of attaching an implant to someone's spine. Could I do it? Of course. Even with basic tools, a spinal upgrade presented little challenge to me. Reversing paralysis was tricky work, but not upgrades.

The more important question chased it. Could I get out tonight? Maybe.

[DocSoo: What kind of implant is it?]

[Splice: Type 2-X nerve mesh]

[DocSoo: Those are illegal.] The moment I sent the message, I felt stupid. Obviously it would be something illegal. I still knew how to implant them. [I don't have a workspace or tools.]

[Splice: You can use my workshop, and I can get you

anything you need for a share of the fee. We can negotiate later and I can pick you up if you can get out.]

[DocSoo: Give me an hour? I need to find out what the gang is up to tonight.] Excitement pumped my blood faster. I wanted to do this so much it hurt. Granted, I would much rather go back to before that blow job, but this made a good second choice. Establishing myself as a surgeon of quality in DeeSeat was a good first step to getting out from under Misery's psychotic thumb. Doing a favor for Splice was a good first step to getting her to take care of my wristband for free.

[Splice: You have half an hour before she walks.]

Half an hour meant I had to hurry. I thanked her and bolted the rest of my cereal. Snagging two latex gloves, I breezed out the door and beelined for number seven. Delusion answered when I knocked, which made me smile. This kid would be easier to deal with that Monster or Misery. He let me in without question.

"Is your mother around?" I asked, not wanting her to overhear me wheedling her son for information.

Delusion shushed me. "She's still asleep," he said in a low murmur. "Late night."

Considering it was half past noon, I had no idea how

to interpret that. "Ah. I should check on Phantom." I scrambled for the best way to phrase a question so he wouldn't suspect anything or report the conversation. At Phantom's door, I paused and restrained myself from taking a deep breath. That would give me away.

"I wonder if you could help me with something? I'm trying to get into a rhythm here and never knowing when anyone is coming, going, or heading out for 'excitement' makes it hard." The lies rolled off my tongue effortlessly, which scared me.

I remembered my mother catching me in a stupid, worthless little lie about cookies. Miko always knew when I made something up to amuse her. And, of course, Ai had figured out exactly when to walk into my office. She hadn't been surprised when she caught me with Bunny, and she'd tossed the door open in the middle of my climax.

Somehow, I'd never wanted anything the way I wanted this. Or, at least, I hadn't wanted anything this much in a long time. Maybe I could blame my emotion regulator.

"Oh, the schedule here is really flexible. There's a drop every Thursday night, but other than that, it's all pretty loose."

Today happened to be Thursday, which I decided to

rename Luckyday. "Is the drop dangerous? Should I expect to be needed?"

Delusion shrugged as he pushed Phantom's door open for me. "Probably. They leave around midnight. I'd be surprised if they don't want you along from now on."

If I snuck out tonight, I had to be back by midnight. For the kind of work Splice requested, I'd need two hours at most, plus travel time there and back. "Thanks, Delusion. I'll expect to be collected then. Sounds like a good plan to catch a nap beforehand. If anyone gets hurt, I could be up for hours."

"Yeah." Delusion nodded absently.

I approached Phantom's sleeping form and messaged Splice. She promised to pick me up two blocks away at 7:30.

CHAPTER 10

At 7:03, I had one arm inside the sleeve of my new black windbreaker and my new combat boots on. Someone knocked on my door. I froze. Panic surged. I switched on my emotion regulator. My heart returned to its normal rhythm and I let out a breath while tugging the jacket off. I tossed it onto the kitchen counter and opened the door.

Monster gave me the warmest smile I'd seen yet. He offered me a bulging, black backpack made of flexible, waterproof plastic. "Hey, Doc Soo." They'd all taken to calling me that already. "Present for you."

I took the pack, finding it too heavy to hold up, but I could carry it. "What's inside it?"

"Medkit for field treatment. Misery sprang for it, figuring it would make you more useful. I don't know anything but the obvious about what's inside it."

Feeling guilty about my plans for the evening, I kept

my gaze on the backpack. Looking at him would give me away. "Thank you. This is...unexpected."

Monster chuckled. "I told her you'd like it. Do you want to have dinner with us tonight? We're eating in about half an hour."

"Oh. No, thank you." I bowed to him, which made it easier to continue not to look at his face while I lied flagrantly. "I already had some of that canned stuff and I'm tired."

"We gotta get you some real food. Anyway, have a nice nap." He turned and walked away.

Shutting and locking the door, I wondered why he didn't tell me about tonight's planned outing and my role in it. Maybe they hadn't decided yet whether to take me or not, or maybe he just enjoyed the thought of tossing me out of bed in the middle of the night.

I checked the time and grabbed my jacket. Twenty-five minutes to get outside, climb the fence, and jog three blocks. With the supply list I'd sent to Splice, I doubted anything in the backpack would help, but I brought it to the window anyway. On the off chance she hadn't been able to get some of it, having this kit for backup might prove invaluable.

Standing on my bed, I peered out the window. Night had already fallen and a steady drizzle kept the potholes and pavement cracks filled with water. Yellow light from the nearby streetlamp glimmered in the rippling puddles and reflected off parked car windows.

As I watched, a car drove past, its headlights momentarily blinding me. More importantly, I noticed that Misery didn't keep any guards outside. I slid my window open and popped the screen out, setting it on the floor. The backpack went through first, then I jumped up and wriggled myself out. My body flipped over in my zeal to hit the wet concrete feet-first and I landed on my ass with an unpleasant thump. At least it wasn't my head.

I slung the pack onto my back and shut the window behind me, muttering thanks to my ancestors for my room being on the ground floor and not higher or lower. Not sure how to skulk correctly, I bent over and hurried to the nearest parked car. Keeping low, I ran to the end and darted to the next. This brought me to the chainlink fence.

In my youth, I once stood with a chainlink fence between me and a candy shop. My account had a small amount in it, provided by my father so I'd learn about fiscal responsibility. The pull of the shop drew me to the fence. I gripped it with my small fingers. And I stayed there, gazing through it longingly because I saw the fence as an insurmountable barrier. Good boys didn't climb fences.

Good boys also didn't kill their patients.

The cool logic of this thought reminded me that I'd switched on my emotion regulator. I switched it off and felt a surge of raw excitement. Standing on the precipice of doing something right and wrong at the same time, of betraying someone I owed no real allegiance to, thrilled me.

Climbing the fence proved easier than I expected, even with the backpack on. My hands and feet seemed to know what to do out of instinct, and in only one minute and thirty-seven seconds, I set my foot on the broken sidewalk outside the Nightmare Hotel. The building seemed smaller. I felt bigger.

My clock ticked in the corner of my vision. Turning my back on the place, I wondered if I could get Splice to pry off the wristband tonight. Would Misery hunt me down somehow to repay her for the backpack and medkit? I deserved to keep this stuff for saving Phantom's life. Misery scared me though, and she'd made it clear that she considered me her property. If I didn't get back by midnight, I had no doubt she'd jolt the fuck out of me until I crawled back, begging for her forgiveness.

No one hung around the Nightmare Hotel. One block away, I found people. Homeless men huddled in boarded-over doorways. One brave woman in a tight skirt leaned against a streetlamp, watching cars pass. Her gaze flicked over me, then she thankfully dismissed me.

A heavy bass beat thumped in my chest and the stench of rotting garbage assaulted my nose. Keeping my head down, I avoided eye contact with anyone. I passed through a small crowd of people chattering outside a run-down warehouse with electric instruments screeching through the broken windows. Enough alcohol hit the air with their breaths that I could taste the cheap, crappy beer they all drank.

I hated DeeSeat for the low drinking standards and awful music.

Ahead, my salvation rolled to a stop at the corner. Splice stopped her bulky motorcycle and waved to me without pushing her goggles up. Yet another new experience for me today—riding a roadbike.

"Hey, Doc Soo." She smiled and patted the wet leather seat behind her. "That's not a spectacular name, by the way. You need something with more panache."

With one hand on her shoulder, I swung my leg over the bike. "I have to be in bed by midnight."

"Then let's go, Cinderella. Hold on and try to relax. Message me if you need to say something."

Uncomfortable with wrapping my arms around her, I settled my hands on her hips. The bike's engine revved so quietly that I felt it without hearing it. We bolted from the curb and flew down the street in wind so fierce I had to hide behind her. Now I knew why she wore VR goggles on a motorcycle at night.

Watching the world pass by to her left, I saw more darkness than light. The bike swerved around cracks and debris in a street too damaged for cars, then we rocketed up a ramp and leaped into the air. One long moment of glorious free-fall ended with an unpleasant slap of my ass on the seat and my groin against Splice.

While I groaned, she slowed and turned the bike down a narrow alley clear of trash or squatters. The alley offered barely enough space for us to pass through, which made me cringe, anticipating a head-on collision. We turned within half a minute of diving down this tunnel of doom and I lifted my head to discover we'd entered a small room with a concrete floor.

The engine died, shutting off its headlight and plunging us into near darkness. Splice popped out the kickstand and stood while she leaned the bike onto it. "Wake up, Doc. We're here. This is my place."

I stumbled through an awkward dismount with her help. The door we'd entered through rumbled shut, cutting off the pathetic light outside. A shaft of bright light blinded me when Splice opened an interior door. I followed her into a room stuffed full of bins, boxes, tool chests, and a collection of screens set up on stands in a semi-circle resembling those at the mechanic I used to take my car to for maintenance.

Unlike that shop, this one had parts and tools strewn across every table. In the empty space where a vehicle should be, she had a raised cot covered with a plastic tarp. Beside it, a robotic arm held a metal tray full of surgical tools. Three black stands held spotlights high enough to shine down where the patient would lie.

"This is...wonderful," I breathed.

Splice grinned. "Welcome to my shop."

CHAPTER 11

"It doesn't really compare to a nanosuite, but it's more than I could have put together on such short notice." A smile tugged on my mouth and pride swelled in my chest for my own skills.

Splice smirked. "I'll take that as a compliment."

"How did you find all this in such a short time?"

"Called in a few favors." She toggled each of the three spotlights and adjusted them to shine on the cot. "I already had some of it, so no big deal."

"You called in favors. For me." Suddenly suspicious of her, I narrowed my eyes and watched her turn to her bank of screens. "Why?" After all, Misery did things for me too. I rubbed the wristband.

She slipped brown mesh VR gloves on and raised an eyebrow at me over her shoulder. "Because I think you'd be a good business partner. We can become a one-stop shopping spot for black market bodyware. Buy from me, get hooked up by you. We split the money, share the space, and throw off the shackles of our bosses."

"Wait. You have a boss too?"

Splice snorted. "Everybody has a boss down here, Doc. Mine is a lot more pleasant than Misery, but he's still a boss. This is his space and I do work for him for free or he breaks my kneecaps. But he's only the boss because I can't make enough on my own to set up a shop. Not enough business, no thanks to him scaring people off, choking my supply chain, and monopolizing my time. Working together, we can make enough to get our own place and just have a landlord instead of a boss."

The picture she painted spoke to me. Two underground cowboys, bucking the system and making it work for them. I remembered the abandoned gas station and wondered if anyone claimed it. From the way Monster had hurried there and gotten us out, I had a feeling some rival gang considered it their property.

I approached the tray and touched the cool metal handle of the single scalpel. The last time I'd used one had been part of the worst twenty-four hours of my life. Only three hours before that, Bunny had come to my office. I'd wanted to talk about my family, about how Ai had kicked me out, but she took off her dress and poured me a glass of whiskey.

Thinking back, sex had been the last thing on my mind. It all went back to that blow job. Once Bunny did that, I felt like I owed her— No, I felt like I *owned* her.

Soft, blue eyes looked up at me. Her hands rested on my hips. She licked her ruby-red lips next to my zipper. I reacted like any man would.

Had I told her to do it, or did I only think those words? I couldn't remember. But it wasn't my fault. It couldn't have been my fault.

"Doc Soo?"

"Hm?" I blinked until I saw Splice instead of Bunny. "What?"

"Looked like you were diving deep. You probably need that, but not now. Your patient will be here soon." She handed me a small box. "This is the implant, that's your table, those are your tools. Get comfy and let's get this show clanging."

"Right." I stared at the box without moving, not sure what held me in place. "Can I ask you something kind of... I guess it would be personal."

Splice flicked her fingers and the dozen screens in front of her flickered into life. "You can ask anything you want. I won't answer if I don't want to."

I took a deep breath and directed my gaze to the surgical tray as an impartial, nonjudgmental participant in the conversation. Sort of. "Have you ever given someone a blow job without them asking for it?"

During the long pause that followed, I tried to recall more details of that encounter with Bunny. One part obviously stood out in my memory. How we ended up that way seemed fuzzy and vague, as if I'd made an effort to forget without realizing it. I couldn't remember the moments leading up to her kneeling in front of me.

Bunny had come to my office to talk to me about her husband's procedure. She didn't understand it and wanted me to explain in detail, or so she'd said. I told her about hip replacement. Somewhere along the way, she had interrupted me and steered the conversation toward what a dick she thought Arthur was. And then she knelt in front of me.

"You're right," Splice finally said, startling me out of the memory. "That is kind of a personal question. Also? Not the kind of thing you usually ask someone you just met. I've been in your brain Doc, but not like that. Since you asked, though, I'm guessing that's how you cheated on your wife and now you're looking for some kind of validation about how awesome you are and how unfair the world is."

Shame burned my cheeks. "That's not— I mean—" My thoughts bashed around, smashing each other into incoherence.

She snorted. "You're a doctor. A shit-hot doctor from what I understand. With a lot of money and prestige."

"How did you—"

"Don't worry, Dr. Tsukuda, your identity is safe with me. Misery let it slip and I looked you up. Your wife is fifteen flavors of pissed at you." She sounded so offhand and flippant. I glanced at her and saw she had her back to me as she flicked her fingers to control the screens. Schematic diagrams showed pieces of what appeared to be a disassembled device.

"The point is," she continued, "you and some woman in your office? It would take a lot of power on her part to make you equals, let alone superior to you. You were the top in that situation, so it was your job not to fuck her. Doesn't matter what she wanted, what she did or didn't ask for, or how good it was. You knew better and you banged her anyway. You're the bad guy in that story."

My mind whirled. I already knew this, didn't I? I'd admitted it. Arthur Belton died because I killed him for Bunny, a brainless airhead I didn't need for any reason at all. She'd been nothing more to me than a whim, a diversion. How did I go from dancing with Ai in a dumpy coffee joint to killing for a toy in my chrome and glass office?

"But I don't want to be the bad guy," I blurted.

"Nobody ever does. Best plan is to build a wall between you and that asshole. Rebuild yourself. Move on. You got a second chance, Doc. Grab it with both hands and run."

My stomach roiled. I was supposed to be Miko's hero. Instead, I'd become Ai's villain.

"Yeah, there's hope for you," Splice said. "Stuff it down, Doc, because your patient is here." She hurried to the front of the shop, peeling off one VR glove.

"Hope for me," I muttered to her back, mocking the idea. "There's no fucking hope for me." I finally shucked the backpack and set it aside. Its weight lingered, dragging me down. Tossing my windbreaker on top of it, I looked up to see a battle-hardened black woman with a shaved head following Splice into the shop.

I switched on my emotion regulator.

CHAPTER 12

Like I often did after a surgery, I leaned against the wall with my arms crossed, staring at the once-again empty cot, and ran over the procedure in my head. Nothing had gone wrong. The patient had other bodyware and I took care of some scarring for her while I had her spine exposed anyway. The filaments laced through her nerves should run smoother after this.

It had gone well, but I needed to get back to Nightmare Motel. As much as I liked the idea of running off with Splice, the bridge to Misery would drag me down into the flames if I burned it now. Beyond the wristband, I didn't know enough about how much power she really commanded yet.

The front door clanged shut. "C'mon, Doc." Splice hurried through the shop to the back door.

I snatched up my windbreaker and backpack. At my

command, the local weather scrolled across my vision, reporting the clouds had cleared and it shouldn't rain again until tomorrow afternoon. Thank goodness.

We climbed onto the bike while the outer garage door rolled open. Splice slipped her goggles over her eyes and we lurched into the night.

[Splice: Are you sure you want to go back? We make a pretty good team and I can probably get those schematics in a few hours.]

[DocSoo: I'm sure, thank you.]

I pored over her words, re-reading them several times. Admittedly, she'd done a good job using her various robotic arms to follow my directions for assisting me. No arguments, no questions, no hassles, no delays. With practice, we would work well together.

[DocSoo: Why are you willing to work with me?]

[Splice: Because I have no interest in fucking you, and you're not going to interact with the patients much beyond cutting them open. No personal shit involved, so there shouldn't be an issue. Besides, you don't act like a drunk, you act like a guy who looks at alcohol as medication for a disease you can't figure out how to diagnose.]

Her statement breezed past me, which reminded me

that I had my emotion regulator turned on. Though I didn't want to, I switched it off, re-read the words, and considered hitting her. At once, she'd insulted and shamed me. I needed to be handled and worked around. My skills were my only value to her. And to Misery.

Gritting my teeth, I stifled an angry retort. [DocSoo: Okay.]

[Splice: We're almost there. Good luck, Doc. I'll ping you when I get the schematics.]

The bike rolled to a stop one block closer to the Nightmare Hotel than before. A crowd still milled outside that old warehouse, and this time, I didn't have to push through it. I thanked Splice and jogged down the street, eager to be away from reminders of all my failings and failures.

Time ticked against me. I reached the corner of the Nightmares' street at 11:56. Men in dark trench coats spilled from the building, making it difficult for me to imagine a quiet, unobserved reentry. Panic prickled my scalp and I considered letting my regulator handle it. This time, though, I felt I needed to deal with it. Misery could only get so mad if she found out I left. After all, I came back.

Ducking around the side of the fence, I ran as fast as I could to get behind the building. Back here, no windows lined the wall, giving me a chance. I jumped at the fence and pushed myself to get over it as fast as I could. Thirty-three seconds beat my previous time by a lot. Fear put a lot of speed into me, it seemed.

I darted to the building, running so fast I hit the black concrete wall. Gasping for breath, I peered around the corner and watched men I'd only seen in passing climb into the cars and start engines.

[Monster: Wake up, Doc. Be outside in five minutes or I'm coming to get you.]

Too relieved for words, I straightened and took a few deep breaths while constructing a response.

[Doc Soo: I heard the commotion and came outside already. What's going on? Is someone hurt out in the street again?]

[Monster: You're full of surprises, Doc. Bring the medkit. We're going to a regular meet, but since we've got you, Misery wants to bring you along. Something can always go sideways.]

I stepped into sight and waved to the nearest gang member. He nodded to me and beckoned me closer. Happy to comply, I jogged closer and climbed into the backseat of the car he pointed to. Wraith slid into the driver's seat. He looked me over and said nothing.

Trying not to fret about being discovered, I held my backpack in my lap and waited. I focused on breathing until Misery took the seat beside me and Monster took the front passenger seat. Everyone wore Nightmare trench coats. Except me. I still wore jeans and a black t-shirt with my black windbreaker over it.

Misery crossed her legs as Wraith pulled the car onto the street behind two others. Black leggings disappeared into her polished combat boots. "We're going to a normal, routine meet with our suppliers. We do this every week and nothing happens. I'm bringing you because I'd like you to get involved in our regular business so you know what to expect. You stay in the car unless someone needs medical treatment or Monster or I tell you to get out."

"Yes, ma'am." At least no one expected much from me.

She watched the scenery through the side window. "Do you think I still owe you for saving my son, Dr. Tsukuda?"

Her use of my real name sent a shiver down my spine. I saw no other way to interpret it than as a threat. She knew who I was and what I'd done, and chose to remind me of that fact. "No. I'm in your debt, Misery."

"That's right."

"Excuse me, Misery." Monster turned with a frown. "Ikuri wants to delay until tomorrow."

Misery snorted and waved him off. "Fuck that noise. We're already on our way."

Monster's gaze slid away as he focused on composing a message. We bumped down the street while I wondered if Ikuri was Yakuza. Everything I knew about them screamed at me to steer clear.

"He says there may be police complications if we proceed tonight," Monster said after a long pause.

"Give him our ETA and tell him I have another supplier option if he's too much of a limp-dick to handle my business."

I kept my mouth shut and watched DeeSeat flash past. We sped through areas with no streetlights or datastreams, Wraith punching us through the darkness faster than seemed safe. I imagined all kinds of creatures lurking in those dark places, though I knew none of them were real. The car slowed when we emerged from the shadows at the old, abandoned baseball stadium.

Hunks of concrete from the stadium's collapse

decades ago lay strewn on the street where no one had bothered to clear them away. Long strings of jury-rigged solar lights decked the building and its neighbors like holiday garlands, providing tiny dots of white light strong enough to let us see the road. This area had only a few, minimal datastreams to tap into and I avoided them. A place like this seemed likely to harbor viruses. Both kinds.

Our five-car caravan stopped in the middle of Royal Brougham Way with the front car at the edge of a giant crack in the asphalt. Misery drummed her fingers on the leather seat.

"He's running late," Monster said.

"No shit," Misery spat. "Tell him he has ten minutes."

"In the meantime, he suggests we do a sweep of the area."

Misery scowled. She opened her door and stepped out. Without moving away from the vehicle, she twisted one way, then the other. Less than a minute passed before she sat down and shut the door again. "The area is clear. Send five hunting inside. I won't be caught with my pants down, no matter which way this goes."

I wished I had the balls to ask her what "hunting"

meant. Looking out the window, I saw a car empty, five men stepping out with guns bigger than pistols. They jogged into the stadium as a group, hustling around debris and disappearing from sight. For unknown reasons, I gripped my pack tighter.

"He's begging for more time," Monster reported. "He says he's stuck under I-five at James Street until his escort can deal with some unpleasantness."

"Why is he stalling?" Misery drew her pistol.

"He could actually be stuck?" I suggested.

Misery looked at me like I was an exceptionally stupid child. "Stick to medicine, Doc."

I huddled in my seat, wishing I had run away with Splice. At least I knew what she wanted and had no problem with it. Misery acted like she had a secret plan for me and it would destroy me.

"What do you want to do, boss?"

Gunfire echoed from the stadium. I snapped my head around in time to see muzzle flashes reflected on the concrete. Two of our five hunting men ran into sight, checking over their shoulders as they fled for the cars.

"What the fuck," Misery snapped. "Monster, what's going on?"

"I don't know. The grid is shit around here. They're dropping in and out." Monster and Wraith raised guns and stepped out of the car.

"Stay here," Misery said as she also stepped out. They all did me the courtesy of shutting the doors.

More gunfire cracked and boomed all around the car. A brave man might have at least watched. I hid on the car floor, using my backpack as a shield over my head. The gunfire seemed to go forever and I switched on my emotion regulator. I still hid. The implant didn't make me stupid.

The door opened and Monster dove inside with Misery, both smeared with blood. Wraith jumped into the driver's seat as the engine revved. Monster reached back and yanked the door shut. Gravity threw me into the seat as Wraith spun the car and floored it.

"Doc, Misery's been shot. Fix it!" Monster snatched my wrist and dragged me closer.

Still conscious, Misery groaned. In the brief few seconds before Wraith plunged us into darkness again, I saw enough glistening on her shirt to guess she'd been shot two or three times. So much for the trench coats being useful.

"Get her coat off," I snapped, comfortable giving orders in this one type of situation. "And get me some light. I can't work in the dark."

Monster grunted with effort. Misery whimpered. The car vibrated. I pawed through the backpack for latex gloves.

My wristband caught on something and I froze. Despite our exchange earlier, I owed Misery nothing. Sure, I appreciated her paying Splice to reactivate my implant. If she'd just introduced us as payment for saving Phantom, though, I could have arranged things directly with Splice. Instead, Misery slapped a leash on me and turned me into her slave.

Bright light flared, momentarily blinding me. Misery's black shirt glittered with blood pumping out of two ragged, wet holes. I took in the situation and decided exactly what needed to be done. For now, some clotting agent and bandages would be the best option until we could get to a stationary spot. She'd pass out and need a blood transfusion.

"What're you waiting for?" Monster growled.

"Shut up." I bared my teeth at him. Ironically, Misery had made my rebellion possible by having my implant reactivated. "I'm not doing a fucking thing unless you hand over the button controlling my wristband."

Monster whipped a pistol out and pressed the barrel

to my head. "You'll fucking patch her up or I'll blow your fucking brains out."

In his place, I think I'd also expect to be dealing with the frightened doctor who'd crumpled in room ten. This version of me could kill a man in cold blood for something as worthless as a pair of fake breasts with red lipstick. "You kill me and she dies. She'll bleed out in five minutes if I do nothing. And if you don't hand over the button, I'm not doing anything. You got another doc you can get to in less than five minutes, Monster?"

"You ungrateful son of a bitch," Monster spat.

"Ungrateful? Ha! Yes, I'm so ungrateful for being made a slave. Hand it over."

Misery managed a few words between gasps and gagging noises. "Give...it...to...him."

Scowling, Monster holstered his gun and dug in Misery's coat pocket. He produced the button.

I took it and tucked it into my pocket. Pleased with my victory, I snapped on gloves and got to work.

CHAPTER 13

[Doc Soo: I may need an exit strategy.]

I sent the message to Splice as Wraith pulled the car into the Nightmare Motel. Misery was stable for the moment, and unconscious. Monster hauled her out of the car while I ripped my gloves off and tossed them onto the floor with the rest of the garbage I'd created while saving Misery's life. As I got a good grip on the backpack, Wraith got a good grip on my arm and yanked me out of the car.

[Splice: What's going on?]

My message summarized my bold action. Wraith, still as silent as his namesake, hustled me into the building and down the hallway behind Monster. For a moment, I thought he meant to give me a pre-op pep talk in room ten, but we followed Monster into nine. Monster laid her on the kitchen floor, which I assumed had to do with how much easier it'd be to clean than carpet.

[Splice: Damn. Go you. What's the situation now?]

[Doc Soo: I'm about to extract the bullets. I have a bad feeling that once Misery is safely tended, Wraith and/or Monster are going to beat the shit out of me.]

Dropping to one knee beside Misery, I offered my room key to Wraith. "Bring me the bag with all the tools. I need several things inside it to do this properly."

Monster nodded with a scowl and Wraith left. "If you think you're walking out of here, you're mistaken."

"If you think I'm going to do anything else under that kind of threat, you're stupider than you look."

[Splice: I don't have much ability to prevent a beating, but I can come down there and be your getaway vehicle.]

[Doc Soo: That should be good enough. I hope.]

With a roar, Monster punched the fridge so hard he dented the door.

Delusion came running into the living room. "What's going on?" He saw his mother and gasped. "Mom! Doc Soo, are you going to save my mom?"

"Monster and I were just discussing that. I need a guarantee of my safety before I start anything."

"God, of course you'll be safe!" Delusion picked up

Misery's hand and squeezed it.

I gave Monster a smug smirk. Wraith returned and set the bag next to me. Digging through it, I found what I needed—forceps and a scalpel.

"What do you say to that, Monster?" I asked.

"Son of a bitch," Monster rumbled.

Wraith pressed a gun to my head and cocked it. When this ended, I'd need to throw up and sit in a safe, quiet room for a while.

Delusion gasped again and batted the gun away. "What are you doing?" he screamed. "Mom is dying!"

Monster gritted his teeth. "Fine. Patch her up and get the fuck out."

My smirk grew and I dove in to retrieve bullets.

[Splice: I'll be on my way in about fifteen, so I should be there in about a half hour.]

[Doc Soo: Perfect timing.] I set a countdown and paced myself against it. When she pulled up, I wanted at least to be close to walking out the door. My fingers flew.

Monster paced the entire time. Wraith stood as an implacable wall of muscle. Through the door they'd left open, I heard boots in the hallway and knew leaving would be more complicated than I thought.

As I dropped the first bullet on the floor with a clack, someone stopped in the doorway. Aside from listening, I focused on stitching the wound shut.

"We lost six," the newcomer said. "Four injured. They'll all live, but a visit with the Doc would be good."

"Get whoever you can of Ikuri's people. I want someone to interrogate, and I want them now. Take whoever you want." Monster crouched at Misery's head. Patch up the guys before you go or I'll—" He gritted his teeth and glowered at me. "Just do it."

As much as I disliked walking away from patients who needed help, I couldn't let him keep me here any longer than necessary. Every second I stayed here offered him one extra chance to swipe the button back. While I worked on Misery, I trusted him not to try anything. Once I finished, all bets were off. "I'm not your bitch. If they'll live, then my conscience is clear."

"Fuck you," Monster spat.

Delusion stared at me, wide-eyed. The kid had so much to learn about how his family worked. "Why wouldn't you help them?"

"Because Monster won't let me do it of my own free will. I'd be happy to help them if they came to my clinic and paid me. I'd even be happy to do a house call. If I was paid and allowed to leave whenever I choose." I tied off the stitches and shifted to the second bullet hole. Twelve minutes left, which made this possibly the fastest surgery I'd even accomplished. Motivation was the key. "The important part here is I refuse to be a slave."

"I know who you are," Monster growled.

"That's true. All that really does is insure I never want to deal with you again. So, if you're going to hold that over my head, you can bet your ass that when I leave here I won't be sticking around, and I definitely won't take your messages or offer my services to you or anyone referred by you. In fact, I might go see if Ikuri would like to hire me. I'm sure he'd be interested to know whatever I have to say about this location and your people."

"I don't understand," Delusion whined.

"You will when you're older," I told him. The second bullet hit the floor and bounced with a clackety-clack-clack.

Monster stood and paced across the living room. "Delusion, go to your room."

The kid straightened his back and made a fist. "No. She's my mother. I was here first. *You* go to *your* room!"

Glancing up from the stitches, I got the impression

Monster wanted to haul Delusion off for a beating. For the moment, my presence protected the teen. Monster had enough brains to guess I'd stop working if he did anything. Aside from that, he probably wanted to keep an eye on me and also probably still harbored the hope he could tackle me and force me to stay.

Several tense minutes passed with Delusion holding Misery's hand, Monster pacing like a caged lion and Wraith standing stock still behind me. Two minutes to go, I tied the second set of stitches off. One minute to go, I cleaned around both sites with damp gauze.

[Splice: I'm here. There's the small issue of the fence and gate between you and me.]

I taped gauze over the first wound. Monster paused in his pacing. Wraith hurried out of the room.

"So that's your plan," Monster grumbled. "Splice. We should have collared her when we had the chance."

Snapping my gloves off, I sighed. "Is that the only way you can think of to get people to help you?" I dumped the small supplies from the bag into the backpack. They could keep the gauze and tape. The durable tools were mine. "I would've stayed here for a long time if you'd just let it be a choice."

"I'm sorry to see you go," Delusion told me with a heavy sigh. "But I think I understand. Thank you for saving my mom."

"You're welcome." Slinging the pack onto one shoulder, I stood and shook hands with Delusion. "I hope to see you again."

"Yeah." Delusion looked away, sniffled, and nodded for me to go.

[Splice: Anytime, Doc. I'm staring at five gun barrels.]

[Doc Soo: Dammit. Meet me where you dropped me off earlier, I guess. I'll get out somehow.]

Monster crossed his arms behind the kid and I thought I understood the message in his curled lip. I had no exit. Except I did. I flashed Monster a smile I hoped would infuriate him and bolted across the hall.

Wraith had left the door open. I slammed it shut behind me and locked it. Then I wrapped a latex glove around the knob and tied it to the fridge door handle. Good thing they gave me such a tight little room. With the lights off, I dashed to the window, locked it, and made sure the curtain covered it.

I peered through the gaps in the curtain while

Monster shouted with Delusion in room nine. Outside, everyone I could see ran for the front door. They'd get past my stupid extra lock in no time.

[Doc Soo: If you can, swinging back right now would be really helpful.]

I snapped the window lock and tossed the glass pane open. Jumping off the bed, I ducked my head and sailed through the window. My shoulder hit first and I splatted on the pavement. The dozen aches and pains my tumble caused took me by surprise and kept me lying flat for a second before I realized that adrenaline would smother it.

Switching off the emotion regulator saved my life. The wash of hormones cascaded through my body and pushed me to my feet. I lurched to the side and heard the loudest bang imaginable. Something smacked the asphalt where I'd been lying only nanoseconds before. Glancing over my shoulder as I sprinted along the wall, I saw Wraith pointing his gun at me. He fired another shot as I ducked around the corner. It hit the wall.

[Doc Soo: New plan. Meet me around the back.]

I sprinted for the next corner and kept going straight at the fence. When I reached the top, a horrifically loud crack startled me enough to fall into the weeds on the other side of the fence. I landed to the sight of Monster throwing the spiderweb-cracked window open in room nine. Apparently, they had bullet-resistant windows, and it worked in both directions.

He pointed a gun at me through the screen. I froze, lying on the ground, like a fucking bunny rabbit. Wraith rounded the corner, his gun raised.

Both men ducked for no apparent reason. Then I heard rapid, thunderous booms from behind me. Puffs of smoke and debris exploded off the black brick wall. Rolling to my back, I saw Splice screaming toward me on her motorcycle, sitting up and firing a machine gun with both hands while the bike kept going straight.

The sight stupefied me. Of all the things I thought Splice might do, this hadn't made it on the list.

[Splice: New new plan. Run for it in a straight line and I'll catch up.]

[Doc Soo: I like your plan.]

As soon as she passed me, I scrambled to my feet and ran as fast as I could. The gunfire kept popping behind me until it stopped abruptly. Not looking back, I kept pumping my legs, expecting Nightmares to chase me down.

Two intersections later, Splice pulled alongside with a

grim smile and I hopped on the back of her bike.

[Splice: I estimate we have about twelve hours before Wraith talks my boss into letting him in for a "visit." I can pack up my shop in about four hours, but I don't have anywhere to take it that I can get on such short notice.]

The wind on my face tasted like freedom and safety. I took a minute to calm down and noticed the aches and pains building everywhere. My body didn't like what I'd just done, but my brain thought it was brilliant. High on victory, I had an audacious thought.

[Doc Soo: I have an idea.] I sent her a location.

[Splice: I'll check on it.]

CHAPTER 14

Dear Ai,

I'm sorry.

I know an apology won't fix anything, but you deserve at least that much. You were a wonderful wife and I dishonored you with my arrogance and stupidity. I know Miko will grow into a good person because you're a good mother. Someday, I hope you can forgive me enough to allow me the honor of seeing her again.

In humble shame,

Hideo

I set my calligraphy pen in its inkwell and blew on the yellowed parchment to dry it. No one used paper and pens anymore, but Splice knew a guy who supplied retro enthusiasts. Matching the corners, I folded it exactly in half with a firm crease. The page fit perfectly into its matching envelope, which already had her address written on it. For an added touch of elegance, I dripped melted red wax along the seal, though I had nothing to imprint it with.

Finally done with this project, I stood and stretched. Ideally, I'd deliver it myself and catch a glimpse of my daughter, but I didn't think I could manage it without getting caught by the police. Over the past week, I'd resigned myself to the knowledge I may never see her again. At least I could rest knowing Miko lived and her mother would take care of her. The nightmares and random bouts of feeling sorry for myself would eventually fade away.

Leaving the tiny, gleaming office behind, I stepped into the front room of the gas station. It had been scrubbed from top to bottom by a small army of kids delighted to have us on Mead First Rats turf. I passed the envelope to a teenage girl named Little Chimi, our gang liaison and receptionist.

"Thank you for taking care of this." I pressed my hands together bowed to her, determined to be better than the man I'd been two weeks ago.

"No prob, Doc." Little Chimi tucked the envelope into a worn denim backpack and resumed using her 'link to do whatever teenagers did these days. Her curly brown pigtails bounced with her movements. "Should be able to get it there within a few days."

"Thank you," I repeated. As it turned to join Splice in the converted mechanic's bay and prepare for a patient later tonight, I noticed movement through the window. Late afternoon sunshine, a rarity for DeeSeat, glinted off a black SUV as it parked alongside a defunct gas pump. Monster, Wraith, and Delusion stepped out.

We knew they'd find us eventually. We'd hoped it would take a little longer.

"Little Chimi, we have Nightmares incoming."

She pulled a shotgun out from under the counter. "I'll handle it, Doc. Go hide."

I messaged Splice to let her know we had company. "No, I think I'll stay. They aren't shooting up the place already, so this may be a social call." Curiosity kept me in place anyway. Why had they brought Delusion? Did Misery die after all?

Splice entered the room wearing her leather apron and goggles, grease smeared across her face and hands. "Any messaging going on with them?"

"No."

Wraith stopped several feet from the door and held

up his empty hands. I had no doubt he carried several weapons under his black trench coat, so this gave me small comfort.

Monster opened the door and stepped inside. Delusion rushed past him with a huge grin and hugged me. This behavior clearly annoyed Monster. The big man's lip curled as he crossed his arms over his chest.

"Doc Soo! I'm so glad we found you!" Delusion squeezed so hard I couldn't breathe.

"How are your mother and brother?" I asked when he let go.

"Both fine. Oh, cool, you got the wristband off. That's why we came. I talked mom into not being mad at you anymore." He took my hand and set a key-shaped piece of chrome into it. Leaning in, he muttered, "Monster is still cranky about it, though."

Unable to suppress a chuckle, I closed my hand over the key and bowed to Delusion and Monster. "I'm pleased to know we can be something other than enemies."

Delusion noticed Little Chimi and blushed. "Hi," he said with an awkward wave.

"Hey," Little Chimi said, the shotgun held out of sight.

Monster's eyes narrowed dangerously, so I cleared my throat to interrupt what looked like a charming connection between two teenagers. "Thank you for bringing me this gift. I appreciate the thought behind it and will cherish its intent. Should the Nightmares require any medical assistance, consider our door open. Our fees are reasonable, and we're willing to be flexible in the face of dire circumstances."

"You fuck with Mead First, though," Splice said, "and you're off the guest list. Is that clear?"

"Yes." Monster's mouth puckered in distaste. "Let's go, Delusion." He settled a large hand on Delusion's shoulder and dragged him out.

When the door shut, Splice snorted. "Like I trust them."

I shrugged. "Neither do I. Well, I trust Delusion. He has a good heart despite his family's best efforts to destroy it."

The trio returned to the car and Delusion waved before Monster rolled his eyes and stuffed him into the back seat.

Splice nodded. "There's hope for him."

Little Chimi tucked her shotgun away. "He's cute."

Grinning, I turned away from the window to get to work.

[Delusion: Would you give Little Chimi my 'link code?]

[Doc Soo: Of course. Good luck.]

[Delusion: Thanks, Doc. You too.]

Other Books by the Author
as Lee French

Maze Beset trilogy
superheroes in denim
Dragons In Pieces
Dragons In Chains
Dragons In Flight

Tales of Ilauris
sword & sorcery fantasy
Damsel In Distress
Shadow & Spice
Al-Kabar

Spirit Knights series
young adult urban fantasy
Girls Can't Be Knights
Backyard Dragons
Ethereal Entanglements
Ghost is the New Normal (April 2017)

AUTHORLEEFRENCH.COM

The Greatest Sin series

epic snark fantasy

co-authored with Erik Kort

The Fallen

Harbinger

Moon Shades

Illusive Echoes

Non-fiction

co-authored with Jeffrey Cook

Working the Table: An Indie Author's Guide to Conventions

Anthologies

Into the Woods: a fantasy anthology

Merely This and Nothing More: Poe Goes Punk

Unnatural Dragons: a science fiction anthology

Missing Pieces VII

Artifact (November 2016)

About the Author

L.E. French is the cyberpunk pseudonym of Lee French, a fantasy and superhero author. She lives in Olympia, WA with two kids, two bicycles, and too much stuff. An avid gamer, compulsive writer, and casual cyclist, she can often be found on myth-weavers.com, sitting in her BeanBag of Inspiration +4, or riding her bike around the city.